NATURAL WONDERS

Redwood National Park

Forest of Giants

Neil Purslow

WEIGL PUBLISHERS INC.

Published by Weigl Publishers Inc.
350 5th Avenue, Suite 3304, PMB 6G
New York, NY 10118-0069

Web site: www.weigl.com

Library of Congress Cataloging-in-Publication Data

Purslow, Neil.
Redwood National Park / Neil Purslow.
p. cm. -- (Natural wonders)
Includes index.
ISBN 1-59036-451-1 (library binding : alk. paper) -- ISBN 1-59036-457-0 (soft cover : alk. paper)
1. Redwood National Park (Calif.)--Juvenile literature. I. Title. II. Series: Natural wonders (Weigl Publishers)
F868.R4P87 2006
979.4'12--dc22

2006015286

Printed in the United States of America
1 2 3 4 5 6 7 8 9 0 10 09 08 07 06

Editor
Heather Kissock

Design
Terry Paulhus

Photograph Credits

Every reasonable effort has been made to trace ownership and to obtain permission to reprint copyright material. The publishers would be pleased to have any errors or omissions brought to their attention so that they may be corrected in subsequent printings.

Cover: Redwoods only grow in very specific areas, and they are sensitive to logging and environmental damage.

Contents

A Forest of Giants

On the western shores of North America, along the coast of the Pacific Ocean, some trees grow taller than a 35-story building. These giant trees are called coast redwoods. Some of the tallest redwoods are in northern California in Redwood National Park. They can grow to be more than 360 feet (110 meters) tall.

Redwood National Park was created in 1968 to protect the redwood forest and its rivers, streams, and seashore. The park was expanded in 1978, and again in 1994. Redwood National Park now covers more than 112,500 acres (45,530 hectares). It is about half the size of New York City. The park contains 45 percent of the original redwood forest that remains in California today.

Many redwood trees in Redwood National Park are between 500 and 700 years old.

Redwood National Park Facts

- There are three types of redwood trees in the world. One is the coast redwood. It grows in North America along the Pacific Ocean. The others are the giant sequoia of North America's Sierra Nevada region and the dawn redwood of central China.

- The oldest known coast redwood was cut down in 1933. It was 2,200 years old. To learn the age of the tree, experts counted the tree's **growth rings**.

- The tallest known coast redwood was 367.8 feet (112.1 m) tall. It was measured by the National Geographic Society in 1963. This tree was estimated to be about 600 years old. Recently, the top of the tree broke off.

- Redwood National Park preserves about 50 miles (80 kilometers) of Pacific Ocean coastline. In some areas, the coast is rocky with thick forests. In others, sandy beaches, wetlands, and **estuaries** are found.

- Redwood National Park is a **UNESCO** (United Nations Educational, Scientific and Cultural Organization) **World Heritage Site** and International **Biosphere** Reserve.

- The movies *Return of the Jedi* and *Jurassic Park 2: The Lost World* included scenes from Redwood National Park.

Redwood National Park Locator

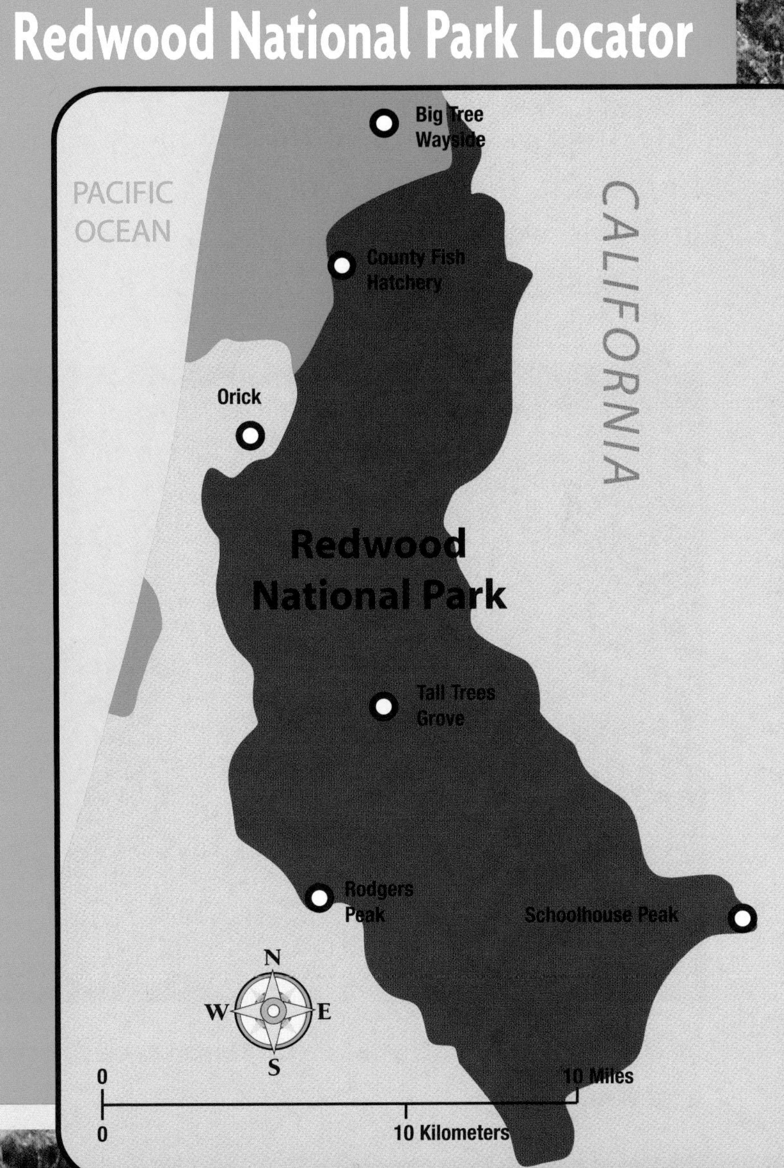

Where in the World?

Coast redwoods flourish from central California to southern Oregon. They are only found within 30 miles (48 km) of the coast. The moisture they need to grow tall comes from the Pacific Ocean as fog in summer and rain in winter.

One-third of Redwood National Park is made up of **old-growth forests.** These ancient forests have remained undisturbed by humans. Everything is important in the old-growth forest's **ecosystem**, whether it is alive or dead. For instance, the dead trees and fallen logs on the ground provide homes to wildlife and plants.

The other two-thirds of the park include forests that have been affected by humans in the past. In the 1850s, logging provided raw materials to settlers, and gold was discovered at Gold Bluffs Beach along the Trinity River. The trees that were damaged by loggers and miners are now being replaced.

In Redwood National Park, fallen trees form habitats for small animals and fungi.

Puzzler

Redwood National Park is just one of the places where redwoods grow along the Pacific coast. There are three state parks as well.

Q Research where each of these parks is located. Then, from north to south, match the name of the park with the number on the map.

Redwood National Park

Del Norte Coast Redwoods State Park

Jedediah Smith Redwoods State Park

Prairie Creek Redwoods State Park

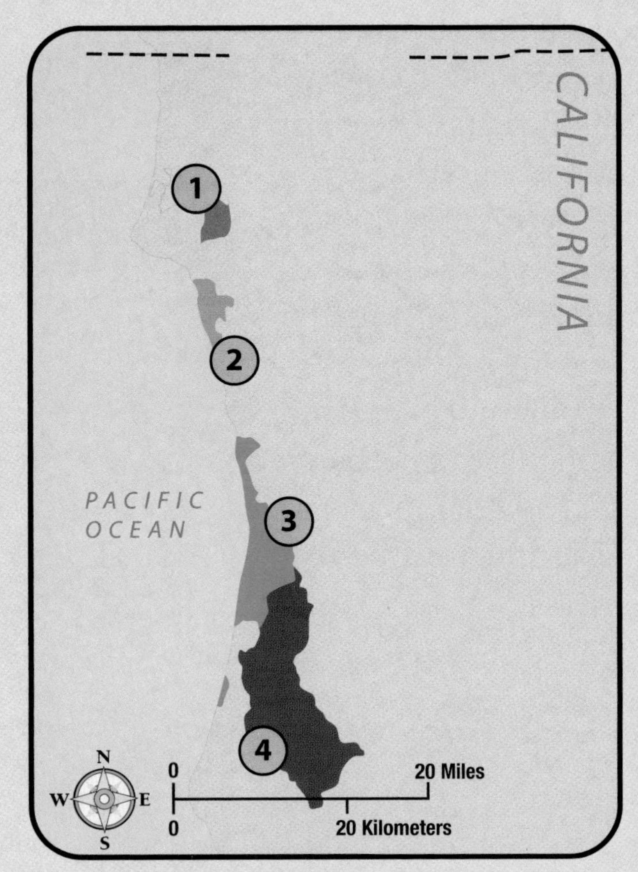

A
1. Jedediah Smith Redwoods State Park
2. Del Norte Coast Redwoods State Park
3. Prairie Creek Redwoods State Park
4. Redwood National Park

A Trip Back in Time

Many visitors to Redwood National Park feel like they are stepping back in time. Some even imagine dinosaurs rumbling through the forests. These forests have remained unchanged for millions of years. **Fossils** found in this area have shown that relatives of today's coast redwoods grew during the Jurassic Period. The Jurassic Period occurred between 144 and 208 million years ago, when dinosaurs roamed Earth.

Redwoods have thrived along the Pacific coast for 20 million years. The coast redwood has been able to survive in this area for so long because the climate here has remained much the same for millions of years. Cool, moist air from the Pacific Ocean keeps the trees and soil damp, even during summer droughts.

Fog is made of tiny drops of water. When the weather is hot, fog provides moisture for redwood trees.

Why Do Coast Redwoods Grow Tall?

Exactly why coast redwoods grow so tall is a mystery. Scientists have developed theories on their growth.

- The trees have a built-in **resistance** to natural enemies. These enemies include diseases, insects, and fires. Coast redwoods contain large quantities of tannin, a chemical that helps them resist disease and insect damage. Damage from fire is also rare because trees are protected by their thick bark and their leaves are so high above the ground.
- Redwoods regenerate easily. Most trees only grow from seeds that fall onto the surface of the forest. Coast redwoods can sprout from stumps or root systems of redwoods that have fallen down.
- The trees live in a healthy ecosystem that includes rich soil, plants, animals, and up to 100 inches (254 centimeters) of rain each year.

New redwoods can sprout from a tree trunk that has been damaged by fire.

Plants in the Ancient Forests

Many plants besides the coast redwood grow in the ancient forests of Redwood National Park. These include spruce, hemlock, and Douglas fir trees. Smaller plants also grow in the park, such as berry bushes, sword ferns, and wildflowers.

Most of the larger trees have tops that have been damaged by the wind. These tall trees generally have fewer branches. Sometimes the trees in Redwood National Park can be damaged by salt spray from the ocean. The trees grow best in groups, where they protect each other from salt and wind.

The leaves on the trees create a canopy above the forest. This canopy stops sunlight from reaching the floor of the forest. It also keeps the forest floor cool. These dark, cool conditions allow few plants to grow. One plant that grows well here is the rhododendron. Its colorful flowers brighten the gloom of the forest.

White oak trees and flowers, such as riverbank lupines, flourish on the meadows and hillsides of Redwood National Park.

Coast Redwoods

The scientific name for the coast redwood is *sequoia sempervirens*. Just as the name redwood implies, the wood of this tree is red. Coast redwoods are among the oldest living things on Earth. They live for about 600 years. The coast redwood is the tallest known plant in the world. It is also the fastest growing conifer, or cone-bearing tree, in North America. Surprisingly, its seed is no bigger than a tomato seed.

COAST REDWOOD FACTS	
Oldest	2,200 years
Heaviest	1.6 million pounds (725,760 kg)
Tallest	367.8 feet (112.1 m)
Average Diameter of Trunk	22 feet (6.7 m)
Average Thickness of Bark	12 inches (30 cm)
Average Length of Needles	0.5 to 1 inch (1.3 to 2.5 cm)

The root system of a coast redwood is very shallow. The roots are no deeper than 6 to 10 feet (1.8 to 3.1 m). This is unusual because of the tree's great height. Most trees and plants have **tap roots,** but the redwood does not.

Redwood trees grow well in groups. This allows the root systems to grow together, which provides support.

A number of coast redwoods growing close together is called a grove.

Animals of Redwood

Many different animals are native to Redwood National Park. They range from black bears and bald eagles to starfish. Some threatened and endangered **species** live in the park. They rely on the old-growth forests, open prairies, rivers, and coastline for survival. Wildlife in the park is protected. Hunting is not allowed at any time, and fishing is only permitted in certain areas.

One of the largest animals in redwood National Park is the Roosevelt elk. The elk were named after President Theodore Roosevelt, who helped save these animals from extinction. The elk herds have now grown to a healthy size in California.

Marine mammals, such as sea lions and gray whales, are often spotted swimming by the beaches. Pelicans, ospreys, and gulls nest and fish nearby. Anemones and crabs live in tide pools along the park's coast.

Bald eagles have a sharp beak, which they use to tear apart their prey.

The Banana Slug

Banana slugs are members of the **mollusk** family. They are the second largest slug species in the world and can grow up to 10 inches (25 cm) long. Their name comes from their color, which looks like a banana with black spots.

The banana slug lives only in moist forest floors along the Pacific coast of North America. Mushrooms are one of its favorite foods. It also eats animal droppings, leaves, and dead plants.

Banana slugs produce a protective coating called slime. This allows the slugs to travel over sharp objects unharmed. After climbing up trees, slugs can drop down quickly on a string of slime.

Banana slugs travel through the forest on damp, dark days or at night. They climb stumps in search of a dark place to hide.

The First Explorers

Some **historians** believe that European explorers saw the coast redwood forests for the first time in the 1500s. Written records from those early adventures are often missing or unclear. This makes it difficult to confirm which explorer first visited the forest. Many believe that those early explorers sailed past the forests, but did not land.

Jedediah Smith was the first explorer of European descent to travel overland through the southwest to what is now California. Smith was a hunter, trapper, and fur trader from New York State. In 1828, Jedediah and his men camped atop a high ridge, covered in Douglas fir, spruce, and coast redwoods. They could see the waters of the Pacific Ocean. In the morning, they headed toward the ocean, but it took them 10 days to get there because of the tangled undergrowth and fallen logs. They were also slowed by fog and rain that made the mud on the forest floor slippery and dangerous.

In the late 1500s, British explorer Sir Francis Drake sailed along the coast near what is now Redwood National Park. In 1581, he was knighted by Queen Elizabeth I after he returned from a voyage around the world.

Biography

Jedediah Smith (1799–1831)

When Jedediah was young, he read a copy of the journals of the explorers Lewis and Clark. They inspired him to travel in the wilderness. At the age of 22, Jedediah joined an expedition along the Missouri River to trap beavers. Soon after the ship left the dock, its mast struck a branch. The boat turned sideways and was swept under the water.

This setback did not stop Jedediah. Over the next eight years, he traveled through the central Rockies, down to the area now called Arizona, across the Mojave Desert, and into present-day California.

In the spring of 1831, Jedediah made one more expedition. While looking for water on the Santa Fe Trail, he was killed by Comanche warriors.

Jedediah Smith Redwoods State Park was named for the early explorer who ventured through much of California's interior.

Facts of Life

Born: January or June 1799

Hometown: Bainbridge, New York State

Occupation: Explorer, Hunter, Fur Trader

Died: May 1831

The Big Picture

At least 12 species of redwoods have been found as fossils in Europe, Asia, and North America. Scientists believe redwoods were common in these areas until about 20 million years ago. Then, most of the redwood trees were destroyed when giant glaciers, or rivers of ice, migrated south during the Ice Age, which lasted until about 10,000 years ago. Only the trees located in the warmest climates survived. Today, there are only three species of redwoods remaining.

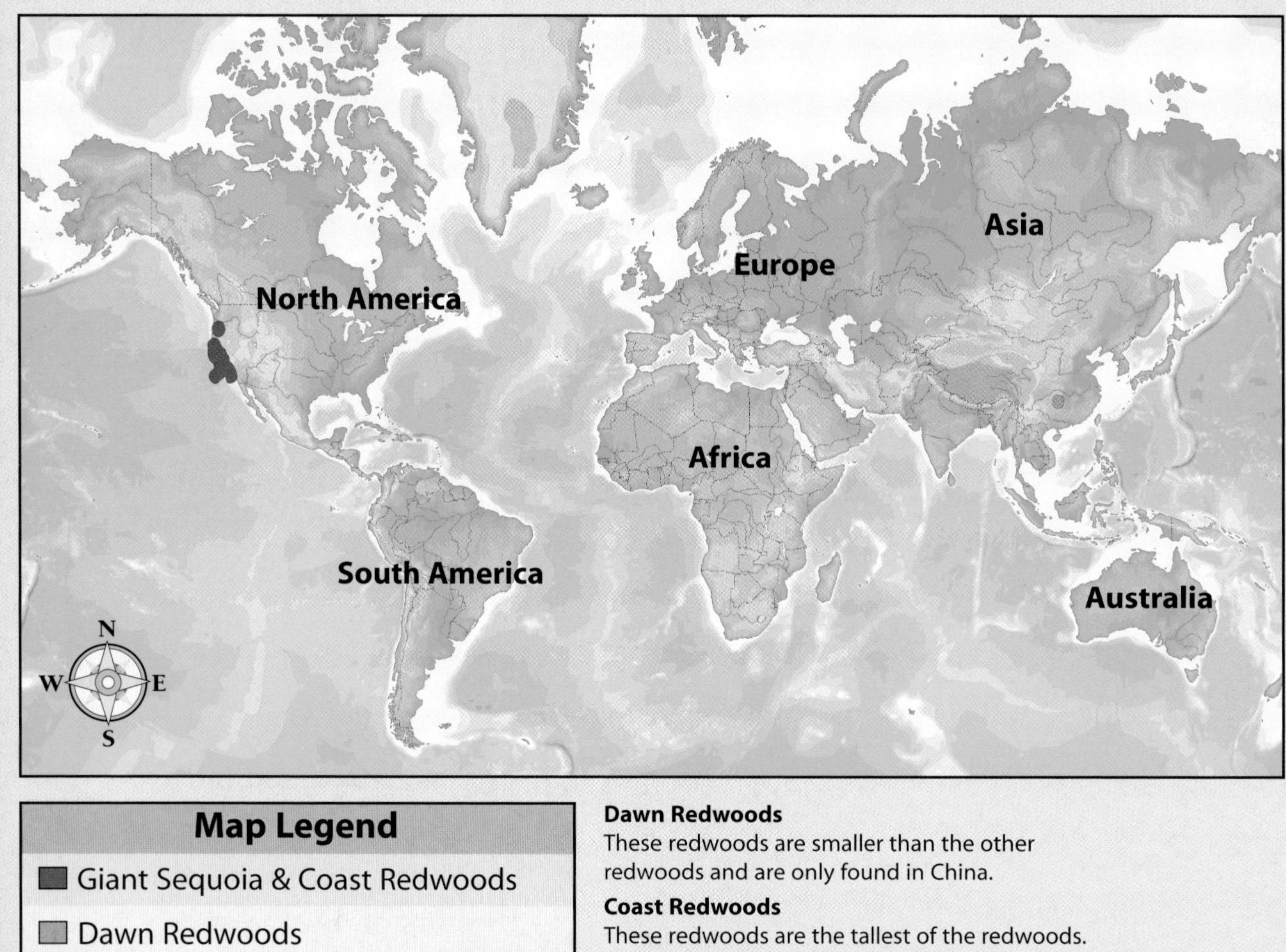

Map Legend

- Giant Sequoia & Coast Redwoods
- Dawn Redwoods

Dawn Redwoods
These redwoods are smaller than the other redwoods and are only found in China.

Coast Redwoods
These redwoods are the tallest of the redwoods.

Giant Sequoias
These are the massive redwoods. Their diameter can be up to 30 feet (9m).

Comparing Redwoods

Height in Feet

360
330
300
270
240
210
180
150
120
90
60
30
0

Dawn Redwood
Giant Sequoia
Coast Redwood

	Dawn Redwood	Giant Sequoia	Coast Redwood
Height	to 100 feet (30.5 m)	to 311 feet (94.8 m)	to 367.8 feet (112.1 m)
Base	to 8 feet (2.4 m) in diameter	to 30 feet (9.1 m) in diameter	to 22 feet (6.7 m) in diameter
Age	to 4,000 years	to 3,200 years	to 2,000 years

Early People of the Forests

American Indians made the redwood forests their home for thousands of years before European explorers arrived. Many lived in small villages along the coast and major rivers. Their food sources included deer, elk, nuts, berries, and seeds. They also fished in the ocean, rivers, and streams.

The area now called Redwood National Park was inhabited by several different American Indian groups. The Tolowa lived in the north, while the Yurok resided in the central part of the region. The Chilula lived inland. They all lived in harmony with nature. Nature provided them with food, clothing, housing, and transportation.

Life for these groups changed when gold miners and loggers arrived. The American Indians were forced to leave so the newcomers could mine for gold and log the trees.

American Indians collected food from the forests, including huckleberries.

Using Nature to Survive

American Indians adapted to their environment. They used the materials they found in the forests to build homes and to help them hunt and fish.

Homes in this region were usually built of planks split from fallen redwoods. American Indians believed that a house was a living being. They saw the redwood planks that formed the house as the body of one of the Spirit Beings. Spirit Beings were believed to be a godly race that existed before the time of humans.

The Yurok were dependent on water. Each family had a redwood canoe that they used to catch fish and eels. Not only was the wood plentiful, it also resisted insect damage and rotting. Trees that had been damaged by lightning or strong winds were used for canoe-making. Often the logs would be left to dry in a cool, shady place for up to a year. When carving began, the hard center of the tree became the bottom of the canoe.

American Indians of the Pacific coast discovered that tall, straight redwoods made ideal timber for building houses and canoes.

Saving the Forests

At one time, 2 million acres (809,400 ha) of old-growth forests existed along the Pacific coast. When settlers came west, they needed raw materials. Coast redwoods were logged to make lumber for homes and businesses. By about 1910, the last of the old-growth forests were about to disappear. Many people did not want this to happen because fossil records showed that these trees were related to trees millions of years old.

To save the trees, a group called Save-the-Redwoods League was started in 1918. The league bought large areas of the redwood forests in order to save the trees from disappearing completely. The State of California helped the league by also buying old-growth forests. By 1960, more than 100,000 acres (40,500 ha) had been preserved.

Inside Redwood National Park, areas that were logged in the past are now being replanted.

Becoming a National Park

In 1968, the United States Congress approved 58,000 acres (23,500 ha) of the land bought by the Save-the-Redwoods League to be made into a national park. Redwood National Park was later expanded to its present size.

In 1980, the park became a UNESCO World Heritage Site. These sites are chosen for their importance to humans. Sites include forests, mountain ranges, lakes, deserts, buildings, and cities.

In 1983, the park was named an International Biosphere Reserve by UNESCO. These reserves are created to promote a balance between humans and the biosphere. Reserves must consist of land, coast, or marine ecosystems.

Visitors to Redwood National Park can stand on the stump of a giant sequoia and admire the giant trees around them.

Natural Attractions

At all times of the year, visitors can explore and enjoy the natural wonders of Redwood National Park. Most tourists visit the park in summer, when the weather is the warmest. The most popular activities are backpacking, biking, hiking, boating, rafting, and horseback riding. Visitors especially enjoy being in the redwood groves in the morning, when the tall trees are surrounded by fog.

Hiking through Redwood National Park can be a breathtaking experience. The park has more than 200 miles (322 km) of trails. Some trails are down at sea level, while others climb to 3,000 feet (915 m) with wonderful views. The trails weave through beaches, prairies, and old-growth forests. Bird- and wildlife-watching are popular pastimes while hiking.

Redwood National Park trails are often wet and slippery. Hikers should bring rain gear.

Be Prepared

Trails in the park are accessible year-round because of the mild climate of the area. However, hikers must be careful because the trails are often wet and slippery. In winter, some trails may be difficult to use. Sturdy footwear and rain gear should be worn in the park.

When on the trails, care must be taken around some of the animals in the park. Although not seen very often, black bears roam freely in the park, especially around Redwood Creek. They enjoy eating acorns and will travel far to find them.

TIP: When camping, store certain items high off the ground so as not to attract bears. Place all food, scented items (such as soap, toothpaste, and lotions), and garbage in a tree. Ensure they are at least 12 feet (3.6 m) up, 10 feet (3 m) out from the trunk, and 5 feet (1.5 m) down from the branch.

Mountain lions, or cougars, live in Redwood National Park. These animals prefer to avoid humans. Sometimes spotted in picnic areas and along trails and roads, mountain lions once ranged from northern Canada to South America and from coast to coast. Now, because of hunting and a loss of forests, mountain lions have a smaller range.

TIP: Although no human has ever been attacked by a mountain lion in the park, hikers should be prepared. They should not hike alone, and children should not run ahead on trails.

Logging the Redwoods

When settlers moved west in the 1800s, they needed raw material for building homes and businesses. Logging companies followed the settlers westward. With demand high, many companies struggled to deliver timber to settlers. Timber harvesting quickly became the top industry in the west.

Coast redwoods provided an easy supply of wood. The size and straightness of the huge trees made them excellent for timber. The redwoods were known for being durable and easy to use. By 1853, nine sawmills were located in Eureka, California. Large-scale logging was everywhere. At first, axes and saws were used to bring down the trees. Then, improved technology allowed more trees to be harvested in less time. Moving the massive logs to the mills also became easier as trains replaced horses and oxen.

Often, logged redwoods are floated down a river to a lumber mill, where they are made into timber for building.

The once large forests of coast redwoods began disappearing rapidly. The 2 million acres (809,400 ha) of old-growth forests were becoming much smaller. Today, only 85,000 acres (34,400 ha) of old-growth redwood forests remain. Of that area, 55 percent is outside Redwood National Park.

Should the remaining old-growth forests outside the park be protected?

YES	NO
When ancient trees are cut down, it takes 600 years for them to be replaced. Countless animal species may be wiped out when the trees are removed.	The number of humans living on the west coast of North America continues to grow. Their need for building materials, including wood, has to be met.
Preserving the forests and establishing parks, hiking trails, and other tourist activities will provide jobs to the region.	Harvesting timber and replanting areas that have been cut down also brings industry and jobs to the region.
Replanting with new trees replaces the trees that have been removed, but old-growth forests can never be returned to their original condition.	Coast redwoods are a renewable resource. After trees have been removed, new ones can be planted.
The loss of trees and undergrowth can cause soil erosion. Damage from erosion can be extensive, especially since the area receives up to 100 inches (254 cm) of rain each year.	Clearing land for logging roads provides access to remote areas.

Timeline

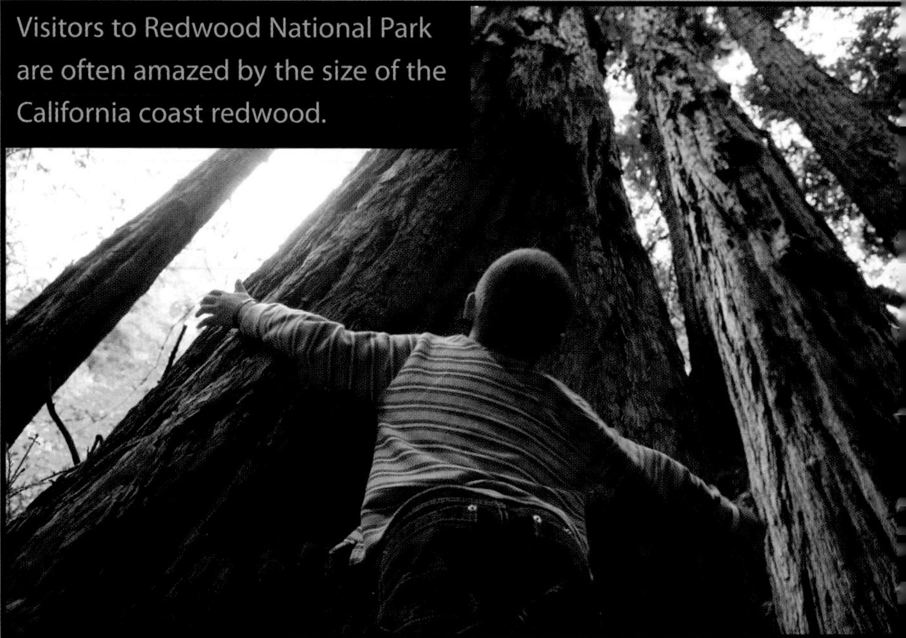

Visitors to Redwood National Park are often amazed by the size of the California coast redwood.

Brown pelicans can be seen along the coast of Redwood National Park.

160 million years ago
Relatives of the coast redwood live during the Jurassic Period.

20 million years ago
The earliest coast redwoods begin growing on the west coast of North America.

3,000 years ago
American Indians begin living in the redwood forests.

2,000 years ago
The oldest known coast redwoods in the park today are seedlings.

1828
Jedediah Smith becomes the first explorer of European descent to extensively travel the redwood forests.

1850
Gold is found along Trinity River, prompting a gold rush in the redwood forest.

1850s
Logging of the coast redwood forests begins.

1918
The Save-the-Redwoods League is established.

1920s
The Jedediah Smith, Del Norte Coast, and Prairie Creek Redwoods State Parks are established by the state of California.

Giant sequoias grow 1 to 2 feet (0.3 to 0.6 m) in height each year until they are 200 to 300 feet (61 to 91 m) tall.

1923
A highway is built through the western section of Redwood National Park. The highway is now called the Old Redwood Highway.

1933
The oldest known coast redwood is cut down. It is 2,200 years old.

1936
Prairie Creek Fish Hatchery is built to support the local fishing industry.

1967
The tallest known coast redwood is measured at 367.8 feet (112.1 m).

1968
Redwood National Park is created by U.S. Congress.

1978
Redwood National Park is expanded.

1980
Redwood National Park is named a World Heritage Site by UNESCO.

1983
Redwood National Park is named an International Biosphere Reserve by UNESCO.

1994
The Jedediah Smith, Del Norte Coast, and Prairie Creek Redwoods State Parks are combined with Redwood National Park.

What Have You Learned?

True or False?

Decide whether the following statements are true or false. If the statement is false, make it true.

1. Redwood National Park is located in northern Oregon.
2. Coast redwoods grow within 30 miles (48 km) of the Pacific Ocean.
3. The bark on a coast redwood is 36 inches (91 cm) thick.
4. Kennedy elk are the largest animals in the park.
5. Redwood National Park became an International Biosphere Reserve in 1983.

ANSWERS

1. False. Redwood National Park is located in northern California.
2. True
3. False. The bark on a coast redwood is 12 inches (30 cm) thick.
4. False. Roosevelt elk are the largest animals in the park.
5. True

Short Answer

Answer the following questions using information from the book.

1. What are the names of the state parks that also protect redwoods?
2. What are the names of the three redwood trees that grow in the world today?
3. What did American Indians use coast redwoods for in the past?
4. What other trees grow in Redwood National Park?
5. How deep are the roots on a coast redwood?

ANSWERS

1. Jedediah Smith, Del Norte Coast, and Prairie Creek Redwoods State Parks
2. Coast redwood, giant sequoia, and dawn redwood
3. Houses and canoes
4. Spruce, hemlock, and Douglas fir
5. 6 to 10 feet (1.8 to 3.1 m)

Multiple Choice

Choose the best answer for the following questions.

1. How many acres does Redwood National Park cover?
   a) 112,500 acres (45,530 ha)
   b) 212,500 acres (86,000 ha)
   c) 312,500 acres (126,470 ha)
   d) 412,500 acres (166,940 ha)

2. In what year was the Save-the-Redwood League formed?
   a) 1828
   b) 1850
   c) 1918
   d) 1968

3. When camping in the park, food should be
   a) placed on a picnic table away from your tent
   b) placed high in a tree
   c) stored in your tent
   d) left on the ground

4. The diameter of the coast redwood averages
   a) 12 feet (3.7 m)
   b) 16 feet (4.9 m)
   c) 19 feet (5.8 m)
   d) 22 feet (6.7 m)

ANSWERS

1. a
2. c
3. b
4. d

Find Out for Yourself

Books

Barbour, Michael G. (editor). *Coast Redwood: A Natural and Cultural History*. Los Olivos, California: Cachuma Press, 2001.

Nystrom, Andrew D. *Giants in the Earth: The California Redwoods.* Berkeley, California: Heyday Books, 2001.

Sullivan, Jenna M. and Sullivan, Laura C. *Kids' Guide to the National Parks of California and Oregon—Written by Kids for Kids.* Corvallis, Oregon: E&S Geographic and Information Services, 2001.

Websites

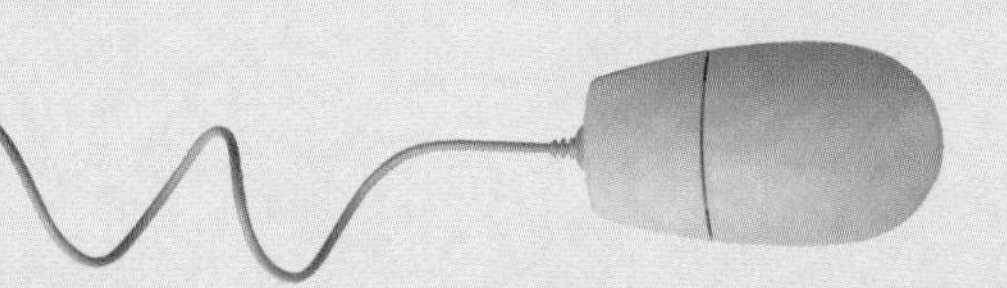

Use the Internet to find out more about the people, plants, animals, and geology of the Redwood National Park.

National Park Services: Redwood
www.nps.gov/redw
The National Park Service offers an online travel guide to the park. It includes information for families and interesting classroom activities for kids.

Redwood National Park
www.redwood.national-park.com
This site provides information for assistance in planning trips, vacations, and obtaining data about the park.

Park Vision: Redwood National Park
www.shannontech.com/ParkVision/Redwood/Redwood.html
Park Vision is an online catalog of photographs and information about Redwood National Park.

Skill Matching Page

What did you learn? Look at the questions in the "Skills" column. Compare them to the page number of the answers in the "Page" column. Refresh your memory by reading the "Answer" column below.

SKILLS	ANSWER	PAGE
What facts did I learn from this book?	I learned that the coast redwood is the tallest living plant in the world.	11
What skills did I learn?	I learned how to read maps.	5, 7, 16–17
What activities did I do?	I answered the questions in the quiz.	28–29
How can I find out more?	I can read the books and visit the websites from the Find Out for Yourself page.	30
How can I get involved?	I can help save the coast redwood by helping to replant the forests.	25

Glossary

biosphere: the areas of Earth's crust and atmosphere occupied by living organisms
ecosystem: a community of organisms and the environment in which they live
estuaries: the mouth of rivers where they flow into the ocean
fossils: imprints of prehistoric plants or animals in rocks
growth rings: layers of wood developed during a tree's annual period of growth
historians: people who study history
mollusk: a species of animal that has a soft body and no visible skeleton
old-growth forests: ancient forests that have not been damaged by humans
resistance: the ability to resist or fight off
species: a specific group of plants or animals that share the same characteristics
tap roots: large, tapered roots growing downward from plants
UNESCO World Heritage Site: a place that is of natural or cultural importance to the entire world. UNESCO is an abbreviation for United Nations Educational, Scientific, and Cultural Organization.

Index